D0054252

Craftily EVER AFTER

- - The Un-Friendship Bracelet - -

By Martha Maker   Illustrated by Xindi Yan

LITTLE SIMON
New York   London   Toronto   Sydney   New Delhi

LITTLE SIMON

An imprint of Simon & Schuster Children's Publishing Division

1230 Avenue of the Americas, New York, New York 10020

First Little Simon hardcover edition March 2018

Copyright © 2018 by Simon & Schuster, Inc.

All rights reserved, including the right of reproduction in whole or in part in any form.

LITTLE SIMON is a registered trademark of Simon & Schuster, Inc.,

and associated colophon is a trademark of Simon & Schuster, Inc.

For information about special discounts for bulk purchases, please contact Simon & Schuster Special Sales at 1-866-506-1949 or business@simonandschuster.com.

The Simon & Schuster Speakers Bureau can bring authors to your live event.

For more information or to book an event contact the Simon & Schuster Speakers Bureau at 1-866-248-3049 or visit our website at www.simonspeakers.com.

Designed by Laura Roode

The text of this book was set in Caecilia.

Manufactured in the United States of America 0218 FFG

2 4 6 8 10 9 7 5 3 1

Cataloging-in-Publication Data is available for this title from the Library of Congress.

ISBN 978-1-5344-0908-8 (hc)

ISBN 978-1-5344-0907-1 (pbk)

ISBN 978-1-5344-0909-5 (eBook)

CONTENTS

CHAPTER
1

Meet MAD-ILY

"Emily! I missed you so much!"

Maddie Wilson ran across the classroom and swept Emily Adams into a huge hug. Emily had only been away at her grandparents' house for the weekend, but for best friends who called themselves "MAD-ILY," two days could feel like forever.

"You too!" Emily said. She pulled back and looked Maddie up and down. "Did you get new . . . everything?" she asked.

Maddie laughed. "Nope, I just made some updates. Remember my 'painting pants'?"

Emily nodded. She and Maddie had clothing they always wore when they were crafting.

Maddie spun in a circle. "Ta-da!"

Emily couldn't believe it. The jeans that used to have streaks and splotches of paint all over were now bright green. And instead of the streaks and splotches, there were now patches and buttons! Maddie explained that she had bleached the jeans, dyed them green, and then sewn on all the accessories.

"So cool," Emily replied.

Unlike Maddie, Emily was happiest in her overalls. Instead of accessories, they had a million pockets for her tools and tidbits.

Although their outfits were different, they had one thing in common: matching friendship bracelets. The girls had made them together, and they never took the bracelets off their wrists.

Just then the bell rang. Emily and Maddie scrambled to take their seats. Emily sat between Maddie and a boy named Sam Sharma. Sam was pretty quiet, but Emily knew he liked to draw. She knew

because occasionally she'd peek over at his notebook. It was always filled with doodles and drawings. He drew everything from robots to giraffes to spaceships—he even created entire worlds.

Emily was about to tell Sam she loved the forest he was drawing when Ms. Gibbons, their teacher, entered the room.

With her was a girl Emily and Maddie had never seen before. The girl had short dark hair, big brown eyes, and a purple backpack that had numbers and symbols written all over it.

"Class," said Ms. Gibbons, "I'd like you to meet Isabella Diaz. She's a new student here at Birding Creek Elementary, and she'll be joining our class. Let's all do our best to make Isabella feel welcome."

The new girl smiled shyly and

then whispered something to Ms. Gibbons.

"Of course," replied Ms. Gibbons. "Isabella just told me that she goes by Bella, so please, everyone, make *Bella* feel welcome. Bella, why don't you take the seat next to Maddie? Raise your hand, Maddie."

Maddie waved enthusiastically, and Bella went to sit down. "Cool backpack," Emily heard Maddie whisper. "And I love your key chain."

Emily was about to chime in when she heard Bella whisper back, "Thanks. I made it."

"No way," said Maddie. "Can you show me how?"

"Sure!" said Bella.

Emily looked down at her friendship bracelet and twirled it on her wrist. She knew Maddie was just being friendly and doing what Ms. Gibbons had asked. And Bella seemed nice enough.

No one could come between MAD-ILY . . . right?

Left Out
at Lunch

Later that morning, it was math time. "As you all know, our charity bake sale is in a couple of weeks," said Ms. Gibbons. "Let's polish up our math skills so we can be sure to give customers correct change. Maddie, would you be Bella's partner for math today?"

Emily looked up, surprised. She

considered reminding Ms. Gibbons that she and Maddie always worked together. But before she could raise her hand, she heard Maddie's voice.

"Of course!"

Emily watched as Maddie and Bella pushed their desks together.

It makes Maddie happy to help people, Emily reminded herself. *Plus, Ms. Gibbons probably chose Maddie because she knows I'm good with numbers and can work without a partner.*

Emily tried to be a good sport, but seeing Maddie and Bella whispering and laughing made her heart sink. And her stomach rumble. *Thank goodness it's almost lunchtime,* thought Emily.

In the cafeteria, Emily joined the hot lunch line. Maddie and Bella had both brought lunch. They made a beeline to the tables with their lunch boxes.

"Save me a seat!" Emily called after them.

When Emily finally made it to the table, she was glad to see an empty seat. But when she slid into it, Maddie barely noticed. She was too busy telling Bella about a science experiment disaster.

"No way!" said Bella, laughing.

"It's true!" Maddie insisted. "It just went *fwoosh* and sprayed everything! I was completely soaked."

Emily was about to remind
Maddie of another story when she
suddenly smelled something . . .
amazing.

"Wow," Emily said. "Bella, is that
your lunch?"

"Mmm-hmm," said Bella. "It's
roasted corn salad and a vegetable
quesadilla. My dad is the chef at the

Mexican restaurant El Gallo," she explained.

"You're so lucky!" said Maddie. "My parents can't even make a decent peanut butter sandwich!"

"Neither can mine!" said Bella. "My dad's a great chef, but the one thing he always messes up are PB&Js. It's like they're too easy. So I make them myself."

Maddie laughed. "That reminds me of the time I tried to make chocolate-chip pancakes," she said.

While Maddie elaborated, Emily finished her food silently and stood up.

She waited for a break in the
conversation.

And waited.

Finally Emily announced, "I'm
going to the art room."

"The art room?" Maddie gave

Emily a funny look. The girls had spent years begging their art teacher, Mrs. Lee, to use the art room after hours. And Mrs. Lee had finally told Emily and Maddie that they could use the room whenever they wanted! But the girls always went *together*.

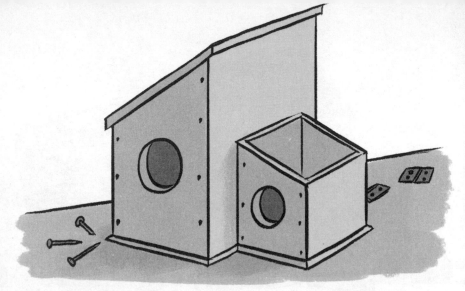

Emily nodded. She was about to tell Maddie about the birdhouse she was building. But just then Maddie turned back to Bella. "Wait. I have to tell you about the time I tried to make tomato soup!" she said.

Emily sighed and cleared her tray. Alone, she headed for the art room.

CHAPTER 3

The *Un*-Friendship Bracelet

The next day Emily brought lunch from home so she could sit down at the exact same time as Maddie and Bella. But once again the other girls chatted nonstop and Emily felt invisible. When Emily finished eating, she went back to the art room.

The following day at lunch, Emily retreated to the art room

even sooner. Mrs. Lee often left the radio on, which made the art room feel extra cozy and homey. Plus Emily was really enjoying seeing her birdhouse project progress.

On Thursday, Emily didn't even sit down in the cafeteria. She just took her lunch to the art room and

got to work as soon as she finished her sandwich.

When everyone returned to the classroom after lunch, Emily noticed something new on Bella's wrist.

"Where'd you get that bracelet?" Emily asked.

"Oh, it's a friendship bracelet! Just like yours!" Bella said excitedly. "Maddie made this one for me. But she taught me how to make them myself too."

Emily's stomach did a flip-flop, but she didn't say anything. Maddie was teaching *Bella* how to make friendship bracelets now?

On Friday morning the class had art. Emily was adding a few details to her birdhouse when she heard someone say, "Whoa! That's awesome."

She turned and was surprised to see Maddie admiring her work.

"Thanks," said Emily. "I've been working on it all week. See, this is where birds can perch, and then this chamber is for bird food."

"So creative," said Maddie. "Want to get together tomorrow? I was thinking we could make friendship bracelets for the charity bake sale."

When Emily looked confused, Maddie laughed. "Not to eat," she said. "Cookies are awesome, but wouldn't it be cool to make something totally unique?"

Emily thought about it. It *was* a great idea. And she especially liked the thought of working on a project, just her and Maddie. But then she remembered something. "Ugh! I have a soccer tournament

this weekend," she told Maddie. "So . . . I can't."

"Can't what?" asked Bella, coming over.

Maddie explained her idea for the bake sale.

"That's such a good idea!" said Bella enthusiastically. "Do you guys need help?"

"Actually, Emily has soccer this weekend," Maddie told

Bella. "But I could definitely use some help! Let's make a plan later!"

That weekend, at the soccer tournament, Emily felt totally off. *I wonder what they're doing right now*, she kept thinking.

"Wake up, Emily!" one of her

teammates yelled as the ball and several players flew past her.

When the final whistle blew, Emily trudged off the field. Usually she'd average two or three goals per game. Today she hadn't scored a single one. She reached for her water bottle—

And gasped! Her wrist was bare. The friendship bracelet Emily always wore—the one that matched Maddie's, that they'd made together, that represented MAD-ILY— was gone.

Emily searched the field, running up and down it. But the bracelet was nowhere to be found.

You can make a new one, she tried to reassure herself. But she couldn't help worrying that maybe the bracelet's disappearance wasn't an accident.

Maybe it was a sign. Maybe her friendship bracelet was actually . . . an *un*-friendship bracelet.

CHAPTER 4

Hidden Treasure!

When the doorbell rang on Saturday afternoon, Bella glanced nervously around the room. Was everything ready? Was everything perfect? Bella was worried that her new home, which didn't even have all the furniture moved in yet, would look bad and boring to her new friend.

But her worries disappeared when she opened the door and saw Maddie holding a tower of crafting supplies. Bella laughed and led her into the dining room. Maddie spread out her supplies on every available surface.

"I love your house!" said Maddie.

"Thanks!" said Bella. "My parents have been making my brother and me unpack boxes for, like, *ever*. So . . . let's see what you brought!"

"Okay," said Maddie, "I've got my bracelet-making materials, but I also brought some other jewelry-making supplies. And I couldn't forget my button collection—I've made some amazing bracelets out of buttons. Bottlecaps, too, see?"

Bella admired all of Maddie's creations, and the two girls quickly got to work. The afternoon flew by as they assembled bracelet after bracelet in all colors of the rainbow.

"Are you hungry?" Bella asked Maddie.

Maddie nodded. "Is your dad going to whip us up something awesome?"

"He's at work," said Bella. "But if we make popcorn, we can put his homemade spice mix on it."

"Perfect!" said Maddie.

When the two girls had assembled a big bowl of popcorn and two ice-cold glasses of lemonade, they suddenly noticed there was no room to enjoy their snack. The table was completely covered with bracelets and crafting supplies.

"We can sit in the backyard," suggested Bella, leading the way.

As they stepped outside, Maddie noticed a small, rickety structure behind Bella's house. "What's that?" she asked.

Bella shrugged. "I guess it's a shed? We just moved in, so I haven't checked it out yet."

"Really?" said Maddie. "But it could be filled with hidden treasure! Gold or diamonds . . ."

"Or bugs and snakes," suggested Bella.

Maddie shuddered at the thought.

"But," said Bella, "we'll never know unless we look."

The two girls examined the door to the shed. There was a latch, but no lock, so they were able to get the door open.

Bella fumbled around and then flicked on the light switch. The two girls gasped at what they saw.

It wasn't snakes or bugs. It was . . . *stuff*. Ropes, tools, wood, paints, glass jars of buttons, nuts, bolts and other fasteners, bicycle wheels, chains, planters, and so much more!

"Whoa!" said Bella.

"I know!" said Maddie. "I thought there might be treasure, but I had no idea it would be *this* amazing! Look at all this cool stuff! And so much of it. Where do we even start?"

"Probably by cleaning it out," said Bella, running a finger through the dust on a shelf. "That is, if my parents let us."

"Are you going to ask them?" asked Maddie. When Bella nodded, Maddie grinned. "And you know who's going to be just as excited as we are?"

"Who?" asked Bella.

"Emily! I can't wait to tell her the news!"

The Inside Joke

On Monday, Emily got to school early. She wondered if she should have worn a long-sleeved shirt so Maddie wouldn't notice that her bracelet was missing. Emily hadn't seen or talked to Maddie since Friday. Her mom mentioned that Maddie had called while Emily was at the tournament, but Emily was so tired on

Sunday night that she went to bed right after finishing her homework.

Emily looked up as kids filed into the classroom. Bella waved to Emily, and Maddie flashed her a big grin.

"How'd the bracelet making go?" asked Emily when the girls sat down.

"Awesome," said Maddie. "Wait until we show you!"

The hands on the clock seemed to be moving very slowly that morning. Finally the recess bell rang and the girls went outside to the playground. Maddie pulled a big box out of her bag and lifted the lid. It was stuffed to the brim with bracelets.

"Wow!" said Emily. "You guys made so many!"

"And we're not even done yet," said Maddie. "We're just getting started, really."

Emily was about to offer to help when Bella added, "We *would* have made more if it hadn't been for—"

"Marco!" Maddie groaned.

"Who's Marco?" asked Emily.

"He's my big brother," explained Bella. "He said we were making them too small. . . ."

"Because he thought they were dog collars, not bracelets."

"Yeah, he was all—"

"No, no, he was like—"

Bella and Maddie started to talk over each other, laughing the whole time. Emily touched her wrist where her friendship bracelet would have been. It didn't matter what shirt she was wearing. Maddie certainly wasn't going to notice that her bracelet was missing.

CHAPTER 6

Sam's Big Ideas

When Emily slid back into her seat before recess ended, she was surprised to find Sam already in his seat, drawing. Out of habit, she glanced over to see what he was creating.

She gasped. Sam had created a huge, incredibly detailed city of birdhouses. In the sky he had

drawn all sorts of birds. And each
bird had a different kind of home!

Emily tapped Sam on the
shoulder.

Startled, Sam covered his notebook.

"Sorry!" said Emily. "I just wanted to tell you that I like your picture. Plus, I think it's *extra* cool because I'm making a birdhouse in the art room. That's where it is now."

"Really?" said Sam.

Emily nodded. "I designed and built it myself. Though it would be cooler if it looked like that!" she said, pointing at Sam's drawing.

"Maybe I could help you with it," suggested Sam.

"That would be great!" said Emily.

At lunchtime Emily waited for Sam, and then they headed for the art room together. Sam's eyes grew wide when he saw Emily's birdhouse.

"That's awesome!" he said. "It would be fun to paint the base yellow. And you could make both sides of the roof go all the way down, then curve up, sort of like wings?"

"Great idea," said Emily.

"Thanks! But it's already pretty cool," Sam told her. "I wish I could build things like this. I guess I'm better at drawing and painting."

"I could help you with that," Emily replied. She got out some tools, and Sam gathered paints. Together, they worked on adding pieces to the roof. They *did* sort of look like bird wings!

"Hey, can I ask you something?" Sam said as he carefully painted the base of the birdhouse.

"Sure," said Emily.

"Where's Maddie?" Sam asked.

"You guys are always together."

"Yeah . . . ," Emily said, trailing off. Then she told Sam how Maddie seemed to only want to hang out with Bella now. And how Maddie had made a friendship bracelet for Bella. "And meanwhile," Emily continued, "*my* friendship bracelet fell off last weekend and it's lost forever. So I guess it's official: Bella and Maddie are friends, and I'm not."

"Why don't you ask Maddie to help you make another one?" asked Sam.

"I don't know," admitted Emily.

"You should," encouraged Sam. "And maybe tell her you feel left out. Sometimes people have no idea how you feel unless you tell them." Sam was now painting designs on top of the yellow.

Emily stood back and admired their work. Sam's design ideas were really terrific. His friendship ideas were pretty good too. She decided to take his advice and talk to Maddie in the morning.

CHAPTER 7

Time to Tell the Truth

The next day Emily kept glancing at Maddie's desk, waiting for her to appear. *She's probably just running late,* Emily thought. But by the time the bell for recess rang, Maddie still hadn't arrived at school.

On the playground Emily saw Bella sitting by herself with a little notebook.

"Do you know where Maddie is?" Emily asked Bella.

"No," said Bella. "I was going to ask you. Maybe when we go back in we can see if Ms. Gibbons knows."

"Okay," said Emily. She was about to walk away when she saw that Bella had been writing something in her notebook. "What are you writing?" she asked.

Bella looked embarrassed. "Oh, just some calculations."

"Calculations?" said Emily excitedly. "Like math?"

"Part math and part science," explained Bella. "Have you ever made a potato clock?"

"Um, no," said Emily. "Tell me more!"

The two girls huddled over Bella's notebook. They were so

focused on their conversation that they both jumped at the sound of Emily's name.

It was Sam. "What planet were you on, Emily? I must have called your name ten times," he said with a laugh.

"Sorry!" said Emily. "Bella was just showing me the coolest thing. Bella, this is Sam. He's an amazing artist and helped me turn my birdhouse into a bird *palace*. And, Sam, this is Bella. She's a coding and circuitry wizard. Look at this!"

Emily pointed at Bella's notebook,

but as she did, Bella noticed Emily's wrist.

"Emily, where's your friend-ship bracelet? The one you always wear?"

Just then the bell rang.

"I . . . uh . . . ," Emily stammered,

getting up. "I lost it at soccer last weekend. I looked all over, but it was gone."

"Want me to make you a new one?" offered Bella.

"That's okay," said Emily. She knew Bella was just trying to be nice, but what she really wanted was her special MAD-ILY bracelet. The one she and Maddie had made together.

After school Emily's mom picked her up. She agreed to drive by Maddie's house so Emily could check on her.

When Emily rang the Wilsons' doorbell, the door swung open. There stood Maddie in her pajamas.

"Hi!" said Maddie, hugging Emily. "Don't worry. I'm not contagious."

"Where were you today?" Emily asked, relieved to see that her friend was okay.

"I woke up feeling yucky," Maddie explained. "But by lunchtime I was okay. My parents kept me home just

to be on the safe side. And I'm *sooo* glad to see you!"

"Me too," said Emily, and she meant it. Maddie's mom invited Emily's mom in for tea while the two girls caught up.

"I've been feeling a little yucky lately too," Emily admitted. "Not sick, though. Just . . . left out."

"You have?" Maddie asked in surprise. "Why?"

Emily took a deep breath and explained everything.

"Wow," said Maddie. "Emily, I'm so sorry! I didn't mean to make you feel left out at all."

"I know," said Emily. "You would never do that on purpose."

At that moment the phone rang. It was Bella. Emily felt the flip-flop feeling return to her stomach as Maddie chatted happily. But she reminded herself that she'd had a lot of fun with Bella at recess.

Maddie hung up the phone. "Guess what?" she said excitedly. Then she told Emily all about the shed full of treasures. "And Bella just invited both of us to start cleaning it out!"

"Cool!" Emily exclaimed. Then she had an idea. "Can we make one stop on the way?"

When Maddie nodded, Emily borrowed a phone and their classroom directory.

"Hello, Sam?" she said. "Are you busy? There is something my friends and I want to show you."

CHAPTER
8

Crafty Cleanup!

"So, what's in this thing?" said Sam, peering inside the shed.

"You'll see!" said Bella, flipping on the light.

"Ohh. I love creepy, crawly— Whoa!" cried Sam. "This is even better than I could have imagined!"

"It's amazing," agreed Emily. Everywhere she looked there were

tools and pieces of scrap wood, chicken wire, metal, and other building supplies.

"Let's get started!" said Bella. "This shed is not going to clean itself, as my mom would say."

So the kids decided to sort every-

thing into piles. Building supplies in one, tools in another, paints in another, knickknacks in another, and so on.

"Where should I put this sketchbook?" asked Maddie, holding it up.

"Oh, that's mine," said Sam.

"Can I see?" Bella asked. Sam shrugged and opened it to a random page. A jungle burst forth, with tropical plants, insects, and monkeys.

"That is so cool," said Bella as Emily and Maddie joined them.

Sam flipped through the sketchbook, feeling more confident now and describing his inspiration for the art inside.

Maddie pointed out a bright butterfly. "I sewed a butterfly costume for my little sister for Halloween last year," she said.

Bella pointed to some gears Sam had drawn. "I think we have some gears like this in the knickknacks pile. I bet I can figure out something to make with them!"

Emily smiled. This day sure was turning out better than it started.

It took the kids the rest of the week to clean out the shed. On Saturday afternoon a ray of sunlight came pouring through the shed's windows, filling the space with a happy glow.

"Wow, look at it now!" said Bella.

The other three kids nodded in agreement. The space had been transformed. It seemed a lot bigger empty. And all their treasures were sitting in bins and bags, just waiting to be used.

"Hey, Bella?" asked Emily. "What's the shed going to be used for now?"

Bella shrugged her shoulders. "Beats me. Why?"

Emily looked around thoughtfully. "Well, it looks to me like the perfect crafting studio. That is, if you know any kids who like to draw and build and sew and make stuff. . . ."

"We do!" Maddie, Bella, and Sam all shouted at once.

By the time everyone went home for dinner, they had a plan. Over the weekend Bella would ask her family for permission. If the answer was yes, they would all meet at recess on Monday to discuss and draw up plans for their awesome new studio.

Sew, Paint, Build, Repeat

At school on Monday, Maddie, Emily, and Sam ran to greet Bella.

"So, what did your parents say?" asked Maddie excitedly.

Bella frowned. "They didn't like the idea," she said.

"Oh no!" said Emily.

Slowly, the corners of Bella's mouth turned up. "They didn't like

it," she repeated. "They *loved* it!"

Maddie, Emily, and Sam stared at Bella for a moment. Then they realized what she had just said and they started cheering.

The kids spent recess brainstorming ideas for the studio: everything from a chalkboard wall to an indoor swing to a foldout desk with room for sewing and working on a computer.

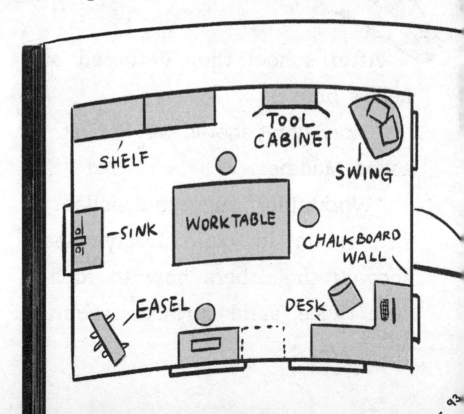

After school they gathered at Bella's house.

"Okay, what should we do first?" asked Maddie.

"Worktable?" suggested Bella.

"I'm on it!" said Emily. She showed the others how to measure twice, sand surfaces, secure

corners, and determine if the top was level. "Ta-da!" she said finally. "Ready for a coat of paint."

"I think I can handle that," said Sam with a smile. "Speaking of painting, what if we did a mural on one wall?" He showed them a sketch.

Maddie clapped her hands with excitement. "I know what else we could make." She pulled out a bolt of fabric. "Floor cushions! To make it cozy, especially when we need a break."

"And how about a potato clock so we can keep track of time?" said Bella. She ran back into the house, came out with two potatoes, and demonstrated how to connect them with wire to an old digital clock that didn't have batteries.

"Aren't you worried we'll end up with *baked* potatoes?" asked Emily with a wink.

Everyone laughed.

Suddenly Emily remembered something. She still had not replaced her missing friendship bracelet. *I'll tell Maddie soon*, she thought.

Every afternoon for the rest of the week, the kids met up at Bella's house to work on transforming the shed into a crafting studio. It was a lot of work: building, drawing, painting, and creating. Sam sketched his mural on the wall with chalk, and all four of them painted. Maddie

pinned together curtains and taught
the others to sew seams and attach
rickrack, pom-poms, and fringe.
Emily continued to build furniture
with Bella's assistance, and Bella
set up her computer. "After all," she

pointed out, "coding is crafting too."

"It is?" asked Sam.

"Sure," said Bella. "It's all about being creative and making stuff. Plus, why else would they call it Mine*craft*?"

CHAPTER
10

Friends New and Old!

By Sunday afternoon Maddie's new painting pants were as speckled and splattered as her old pair had been. Bella came running out of the house with a bandage for Emily's newest scratch.

"Ouch," she said sympathetically.

"Yeah," said Emily. "It was worth it, though."

"I'll say!" said Sam. "This place is amazing!"

The kids admired their work. They had created a Sewing Station and a Coding Corner. The sewing machine was bolted to the tabletop, but you could flip the table up to

create more workspace. Bella had made sure the computer had high-speed Internet by repositioning her family's router. There was Sam's Painting Pavilion, which was lined with all different color paints and about a million brushes of different

sizes. Emily's Carpentry Cabinet
had tons of tools and materials. The
shed already had a working sink,
but the kids had added shelving
for all their supplies. Plus, they'd
painted a chalkboard wall and
added that swing!

"Well," said Maddie, "I guess all
there is left to do is . . . make stuff!
What should we create first?"

Suddenly Bella gasped. "The charity bake sale!" she remembered. "It's in a couple of days!"

"Oh no! The friendship bracelets!" said Emily. "We got so busy setting up the studio, we forgot to make more!"

Sam looked at the girls, utterly confused.

"To sell, not to eat," Emily explained. "Maddie and Bella made a bunch, but we need more if we're going to have enough for the bake sale."

"Well, can you teach me?" asked Sam. "With four of us, it should go pretty fast."

"Great idea!" said Bella. "Here, watch. This is how Maddie showed me." She selected four strands of embroidery thread, tied a knot, and

taped it to the big worktable.

"Slow down!" said Sam with a laugh. But he caught on quickly. He copied Bella's movements. Emily and Maddie joined them at the table and started making bracelets too. Before long they were tying off the bracelets' ends.

Suddenly Emily felt a tap on her shoulder. She turned and saw that Maddie was holding out something for her.

It was the most beautiful brace-let she had ever seen. Emily turned it over in her hand, admiring it.

"The other day I noticed that you weren't wearing your bracelet," Maddie explained. "I sort of figured you'd lost it but maybe didn't want to tell me?"

Emily nodded in disbelief.

"Well, I made you a new one. See? The four colors represent each

of us. And we can make one for Sam, too!" said Maddie.

Emily beamed as Maddie tied the brand-new bracelet on her wrist.

The four kids spent the rest of the afternoon making bracelets, laughing, and talking about future projects.

As Emily tied knot after knot, she smiled to herself. She was so glad she had talked to Maddie about her feelings. The two girls were still as close as ever. And to top it all off, Emily had made two *new* friends! So much for that *un*-friendship bracelet!

How to Make . . .
A Friendship Bracelet

What you need:

Embroidery thread (four colors!)
Scissors
Tape

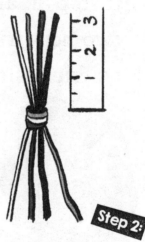

Step 1:

Cut four strands of embroidery thread (one of each color) about twelve inches long.

Step 2:

Holding the strands by one end, tie them all together with a knot, leaving about three inches above the knot.

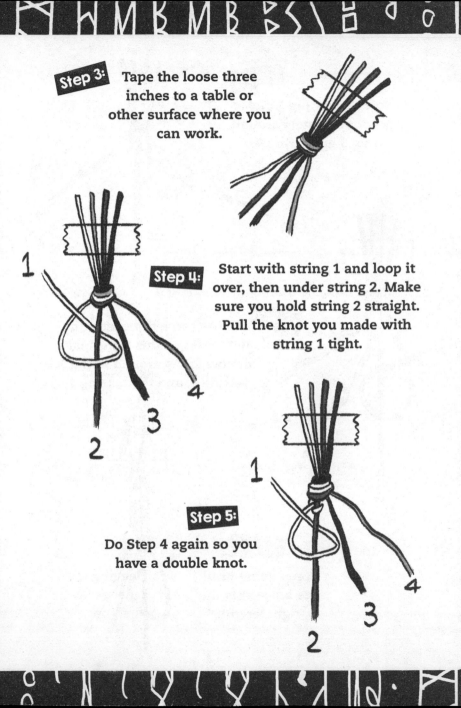

Step 3: Tape the loose three inches to a table or other surface where you can work.

Step 4: Start with string 1 and loop it over, then under string 2. Make sure you hold string 2 straight. Pull the knot you made with string 1 tight.

Step 5: Do Step 4 again so you have a double knot.

1

2

3

4

1

2

3

4

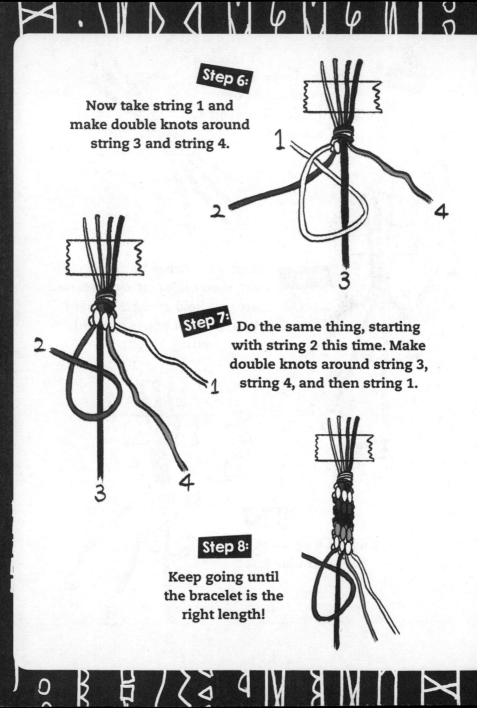

Step 6:

Now take string 1 and make double knots around string 3 and string 4.

1

2

4

3

Step 7: Do the same thing, starting with string 2 this time. Make double knots around string 3, string 4, and then string 1.

2

1

3

4

Step 8:

Keep going until the bracelet is the right length!

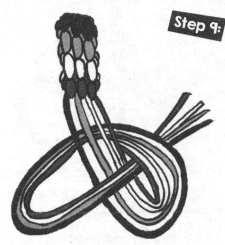

Step 9:

When you're done, gather the ends together and tie a knot so the bracelet is secure. Then trim the ends but leave one inch.

Step 10:

Tie the two ends together to make a bracelet!

Here's a sneak peek at the next Craftily Ever After book!

#2

Craft**ILY** EVER AFTER

- - Making the Band - -

by Martha Maker   illustrated by Xindi Yan

"Should we just . . . start?" Bella Diaz asked, glancing at her watch.

"Let's wait a few more minutes," Emily Adams suggested.

"Yeah," agreed Maddie Wilson.

The three friends were at their craft clubhouse—formerly known as the old shed in Bella's backyard. Usually, it was four friends, but Sam Sharma was nowhere in sight.

Their clubhouse was filled with all sorts of materials the kids used for their crafty projects. They had a Sewing Station, where Maddie could often be found. There was a Coding Corner, with a computer that Bella had installed. Emily's Carpentry Cabinet contained tons of tools, gadgets, and materials like nuts and bolts. And Sam's Painting Pavilion housed different color paints and about a million brushes of different sizes.

But where *was* Sam?

"Sorry I'm late!" someone shouted

as the shed door flew open. There was Sam, breathless. "I had to clean my hamster's cage. It takes forever!" he explained.

Maddie nodded sympathetically. "I know what that's like," she said. "I mean, having to do chores. It's my job to set the dinner table every night!"

"You're both lucky," said Bella. "Since my dad is a chef, he uses every pot and pan when he cooks. And guess who has to clean up? But, the other night, doing the dishes actually gave me an amazing idea for a new crafting project. Behold!"

Bella handed an object to each of her friends.

"Scrub brushes?" asked Sam, confused.

"Right now, yes," said Bella. "But we're going to transform them into: Brushbots!"

Bella opened her note book to a diagram. "A Brushbot is a battery-powered scrub brush that can move on its own," she explained.

"And sort of looks like a robot!" exclaimed Sam. "Genius!"